Lettice

To Dad, with love and thanks for coming to
watch me every time I've tried to be a dancer!
Manny

This edition produced for The Book People Ltd, Hall Wood Avenue, Haydock, St Helens WA11 9UL
First published in hardback in Great Britain by HarperCollins Publishers Ltd in 2001.
First published in paperback by Collins Picture Books in 2002.

5 7 9 10 8 6

ISBN: 0 00 770801 7

Collins Picture Books is an imprint of the Children's Division, part of HarperCollins Publishers Ltd.

Text and illustration copyright © Mandy Stanley 2001
The author/illustrator asserts the moral right to be identified as the author/illustrator of the work.
A CIP catalogue record for this title is available from the British Library.
The HarperCollins website address is:
www.fireandwater.com

Manufactured in Thailand for Imago

Lettice

The Dancing Rabbit
Mandy Stanley

TED SMART

Lettice Rabbit and her family lived high up on the top of the hill. Nibble, nibble, hop, hop, every day was the same...

until the day Lettice saw a picture
pinned to a tree. It was then she
knew that she wanted to be like the
little girl in the picture. She wanted
to be a dancer more than anything
else in the world.

Lettice thought Town would be the best place to find out more, so she hopped there all by herself. She'd never been so far in her life.

Town was exciting – almost too exciting. There were lots of busy people, noisy babies, chatty children and big scary dogs!

Seeing an open door Lettice peeped in – and
there she saw dancers just like in the picture.
  'I want to dance!' she cried rushing in.
  The music stopped and everybody looked.
  'Please may I join in?' asked Lettice shyly.
  'Yes,' said the surprised teacher, 'but first
you must get dressed in ballet clothes.'

Lettice didn't know what to do – she had never worn clothes before.

  'You can get them at the shop we get ours from,' called out a little girl.

At the shop Lettice tried on all the clothes,

but the dress dragged
on the floor,

the shoes were
like flippers,

and the cardigan
was huge.

Lettice began
to cry.

Then the shop assistant
brought out a ballerina doll.

All the doll's clothes
fitted perfectly.

Now Lettice was ready!

Lettice hopped back to the ballet class.
   First, she had to learn the ballet positions.
She watched and listened very carefully
copying the other dancers. The ballet
teacher showed her how to hold her head
high so her ears would look graceful.

Lettice worked very hard.

She turned out
her long toes,

she stretched up her arms

and she tried not to wobble. When she jumped...

it looked as though she were flying! When she

twirled and whirled she was almost a blur.

Every week, Lettice went to Town for
her class and at home she practised every
spare minute of the day.

The teacher thought Lettice was very special and was amazed at her extraordinary jumps.

Lettice worked so hard that each night she went to bed very tired – but happy.

A few weeks later it was the end of term show.
Lettice had been chosen for the starring role.
She had a gorgeous costume – there was
even a tiny crown!

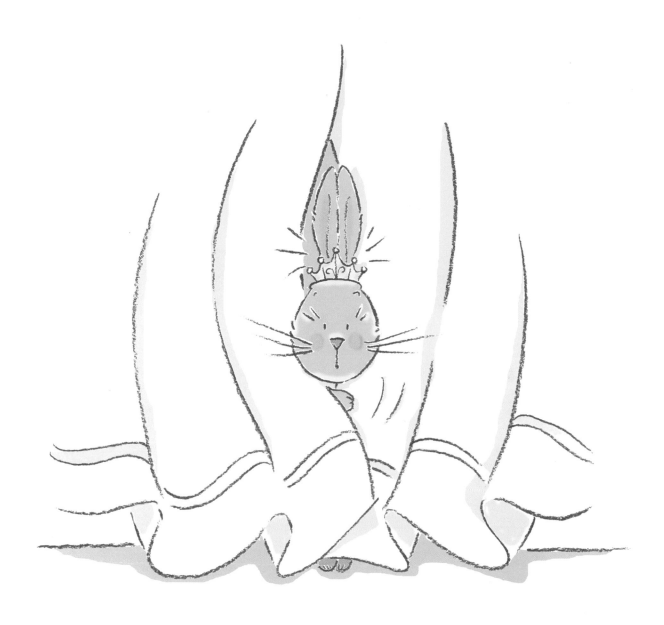

All Lettice's family had come to see her.
Lettice was so nervous she thought she'd
never be able to dance at all!

The lights went down, the music began. Lettice took a deep breath… and leapt on to the stage.

She glittered and twinkled and soared through the air.

The Rabbit family were so proud, they clapped their soft little paws all through the show.

When it was all over the Rabbit family were so excited they rushed straight home.

'Wait for me,' squeaked Lettice, but they didn't hear her.

Poor Lettice, she was tired and alone, and as she slowly walked home, the rain fell. She felt so miserable she just wanted to crawl into the warm, cosy burrow and fall fast asleep.

Next day the Rabbit family were busy collecting apples, cabbages and carrots ready for a picnic. 'Lettice won't want to come,' said her brothers and sisters, 'she's a star now!'

But Lettice heard them and felt very hurt – how could they go without her?

She pulled off the crown, and threw off the dress. She kicked off her shoes and scrambled out of her tights.

'Wait for me!' she cried, and raced up the hill.
She could feel the sun on her fur, the grass
between her toes and the wind in her ears.
It was wonderful!

Lettice had found out what it felt like
to be a ballerina, but she knew that being
a rabbit was, by far, the very best thing
in the world.

Lettice
The Flying Rabbit

'Lettice the Flying Rabbit' will be published by HarperCollins Publishers in 2003.